Visions of a

Skylark

Dressed in Black

Visions of a

Skylark

Dressed in Black

(Short Stories and Poems)

BY ABERJHANI
© July 2012

ALSO BY ABERJHANI

I Made My Boy Out of Poetry (1997)

Encyclopedia of the Harlem Renaissance (with Sandra L. West, 2003)

The Wisdom of W. E. B. Du Bois (2003)

Christmas When Music Almost Killed the World (2007)

The Harlem Renaissance Way Down South (2007)

ELEMENTAL, The Power of Illuminated Love (with Luther E. Vann, 2008)

The American Poet Who Went Home Again (2008)

The River of Winged Dreams (2010)

A CREATIVE THINKERS INTERNATIONAL
AND BLACK SKYLARK SINGING BOOK

In honor of all fellow travelers on the path of love divine.

And for those angels newly-born in New York City, Washington, D.C., and Pennsylvania on September 11, 2001.

"Yet at the core of his perceptions was the key, disembodied in fragments of verse, by which the hallucination of history/hell might be overcome."
--Jose' Arguelles, *The Transformative Vision*

Table of Contents

II. *one river crying and another river laughing*

III. *supremely robed in the diamonds of his skin*

IV. *that's how we ebony skylarks are*

V. where echoes of heaven sighed peace

Introduction

When a reader enters the pages of a book of poetry, he or she enters a world where dreams transform the past into knowledge made applicable to the present, and where visions shape the present into extraordinary possibilities for the future. One of the funny things about those dreams and visions is that although they spring from the heart and soul of the writer, it is not unusual for readers to sometimes see themselves reflected in their light. This is possible because the reality of a serious writer is a reality of many voices, some of them belonging to the writer, some of them belonging to the world of readers at large.

The strange echoes of selves indigenous to a creative personality and of those, one might say, supplemental to it, tend to populate one's consciousness like so many garrulous birds exploding the throat of an otherwise muted forest. One voice might stake claim to a writer's attempts at intellectual authority and by doing so, without realizing it, initiate a conversation with the reader's own sense of intellectual insight. Another might reflect with disconcerting humility on the subtleties of the spiritual universe. And yet other such voices might flutter back and forth like visitations from an alien memory or like panels of revealing light shining down from an upper room of illuminated insight. They all begin with the poet's creative spiritual impulse to mold language and experience into something worth sharing and they continue with the reader's acceptance of the proffered gift.

Exactly what does it mean when a Nobel Laureate such a Toni Morrison writes in a voice of ancestral memory so intense it triggers mystical events in the lives of many who experience it? What should a reader make of Pablo Neruda's voice pouring through the image of a fallen chestnut and speaking from that image as though he were its own original soul? How is one to interpret a given writer's successful abandonment of his or actual racial or gender identity in life in favor of a literary one that is completely opposite to what he or she truly is? The woman or man who is a poet, or fiction writer, or playwright, or all of these, is engaged constantly in a jazz ballet of vocabularies, passions, genders, histories, perspectives, death, love, and life. The music of revelation announces itself to the reader in somber brooding tones or in melodies light as air and one is invited to dance with the most captivating of partners: poetry.

Visions of a Skylark Dressed in Black is therefore presented as a freely-styled dance with readers. It is a dance that rocks to the jubilations, blues, testimonies, nightmares, heartbeats and loveshouts of one creative consciousness spinning and hovering to the music of its own extraordinary flight between dimensions of fantastic being.

by Aberjhani
July 2007
Savannah, Georgia

I. oh glowing bird of midnight love

Birth as Prologue

My suspicion is that I was born reaching for it, the gently swaying veil of light that composes the face of my beloved.

According to my father, I was born some time between 3 and 5 a.m. in a desert on the night of a blue moon in August. He says that both he and my mother were asleep when it happened, that she thought I was him seeking to comfort either her nocturnal agitations or perhaps his own wishes while she dreamed of seven dolphins singing the psalms of David and Neruda to a small star that had fallen into the Atlantic Ocean. In her dream, the dolphins had gathered their voices into a circle around the star and the vibrations of their compassion began to lift it out of the ocean like a command from the Greater Beloved unshackling a soul condemned to hell and lifting it toward a higher sphere. The sleek silver bodies of the dolphins danced like flowers upon the waves as the star rose slowly but ever higher. It was when the flaming ball broke the surface of the ocean that, my father tells me, my mother felt the tug on the connection between us and woke him up with her fists and screams.

What was it that frightened my mother most? The fact that I was outside her body, on my hands and knees covered with the wetness of her inner being and now, too, the sand and darkness and mysticisms of the world? Or that there in front of my eyes still gazing at other existences was a scorpion the size of my father's foot. The arrow point of its poisonous tail was curved towards my face. I believe, sometimes, that I recall hearing it, the scorpion, prophesize that mine would be an existence at once made glorious by unyielding fever for the Great Beloved and yet, relentlessly tortured by that same burning. My father could not move faster than the scorpion could strike. The spear of its tail pierced the space centered between my brows.

What was it that surprised my father the most? The fact that despite the speed of his love he had been too slow to stop the scorpion's poison from finding its mark? Or that this freak of a scorpion nearly as large as I, struck and gashed the flesh of my forehead, then fell immediately lifeless into the sand? Even as he rushed, weeping, to gather me in his arms, he heard a keen high wailing that rippled across the desert like the sudden unfolding of dimensions hidden and divine. He and my mother huddled together, presuming the scorpion's sting had erased my life, hammered like two brittle nails by a screeching that grabbed the night by its ears and shook it until the entire desert joined in its concert: coyotes weeping the names of dead medicine men, hyenas crackling the sprits of mischief and mystery, tumbleweeds whispering poetry against the rising and falling of the earth's sighing breasts, three owls glowing like Sufis with the ballad of a majestic name pouring like wine over the fears of human hearts.

The tears that fell from my mother's and father's eyes were so profuse that he says they could barely see, and yet nothing could have stopped them from witnessing the sight of velvet-black so dynamic with resonance it was radiant. My father recalls a cloudburst of sand, a spiraling curtain of beaded lights, and the sudden appearance of the ebony singer soaring upward, its wings barely moving as it cleaved through the air toward the moon. The higher it flew, the louder it sang, scalding eruptions of harmony and timbre, and the louder it sang, the stronger the aroma of violets and roses in that place where neither grew. The creature sailed in a straight line as if a powerful spirit were pulling it from

2

above. It then stood out in brilliant black relief against the huge round white of the moon, black diamond on white onyx, dizzy and dizzying with the churning spiral of its spells booming through the desert. It seemed for a time suspended inside the moon's adoration of its flight, absorbing through its beauty half-notes and whole melodies, fragments of genius and tragedy. Then it began its journey downward, traveling so fast it seemed the planet would shatter once it struck the ground.

It never did. No more than five feet from solid earth, and less than ten feet from where my mother stood holding me, this feathered creature swooped in a curve and snatched between its beak of sparkling shadow the spent corpse of the scorpion. It ascended in a wide arc that took it once again face to face with the moon, then descended in a wider circle than before, in this way journeying through the eternal night until it was no longer visible.

My father and mother wept until they saw their tears had washed from my body the sand and fluids of birth, and that despite the scar shaped oddly like a crescent moon between my brow, I was very much alive. My father was as frightened as he was elated. My mother was as angry as she was baffled. Not only had I left her womb without assistance, but I had done so three months early. And, she told my father, I had deprived her of a responsibility, and thus a source of honor, that was distinctly hers.

"A male child who delivers himself has no need for a mother. He belongs to you and this desert." With those words she left me in my father's arms. He remained with me until I was 11, when I had grown as tall as he and people seeing us together would mistake us for brothers. He said death would make it easier for him to find my mother and reclaim the adventure of their marriage, but I have spoken since with his spirit and things did not go exactly as he planned. On this side of life my mother had already chosen another husband, and on the other side of death was waiting for my father another wife.

3

How much of what my father told me about my birth was simply myth to entertain a growing boy and how much of it truth I may never know. What I can say for certain is that the scar between my eyes is indeed a curious piece of art, something like a shadow of a kiss trying to complete itself. And my life is constructed out of very odd encounters with unusual beings and entities, strange enemies and allies. But most of all, apparently I am owned by the mystery of the Great Beloved, of who or what it is, of its presence both within and external to my being. Am I a chronicler of its reality or simply one articulation of it? I find in all things, in streets and ants and people and streams and stars, both possible answers to this question, and, further questions that dig even deeper the well of my tortured ecstatic longing.

The Nomad's Vision: Ode to a Skylark
Dressed in Black

I see your wings are made
of many kingdoms,
nations, and stories
oh glowing bird of midnight love,
lovely lyricist
of daybreak and nightjoy.
My knees were two
bleeding bones
painting pain
upon desert stone
when your shadow
pulled the sun
beneath its tongue
of bold dark miracles
and a wave of melodies
scented with ash and rose
covered my head
with visions bright
and wondrous.
Air like thorns
shredded my lungs
and showered my blood
with sugared rain falling
from the whistling cloud
of your wine-sweet soul.

I was on bended
broken bleeding knees
when a Spiritman
dressed in rainbows

came towards me
as if dancing, as if crying,
as if not-fully-born,
he pulled me to my feet
then waved one immense black hand
and scattered my senses like dice—
there appeared upon the desert
an entire city
of pearl-covered domes
flashing knowledge and celebration—
he waved his hand a second time
and a boulevard
jeweled with pyramids
stood goldenbronze
beneath your floating shadow.
In the splendid lines
and circles
of that gleaming city
I witnessed my soul
flying among faces
from yesterday and tomorrow,
one calling himself Joseph,
another saying Arabi,
one calling herself Sheba
and another singing Thou-and-I art-One.
And I looked at the Spiritman
to ask what these things meant,
both of his eyes
were filled with your voice
rolling like drums
through my chest,
he spoke
through the lifting of his hands,
each time they rose
a new city breathed in light

6

and an ancient country
fell to its grave,
I heard no shame
in his song
as he removed his robe
and covered my ignorance,
his fingers traced
"you are loved"
upon my lips
and I walk now
as I saw him walk
partly stumbling/dancing

Lord so drunk
beneath the black fire
of your wings chanting and rising,
my brain staring at the sun
living like a king
inside the beat
of your sweet majestic flight.

Magnetic Black Towards Light

Broken skylark emerging magnetic black towards light
feels pressed against ethereal lips
words and worlds of blue-white enigma.

True lovers earn their genius
in schools of blood, prophecy and dust.
Those who survive death's stern teachings
graduate with honors
from the university of the soul.

When next you open
the emerald book of your heart
read carefully what it says
about the seeds of this moment
and the butterfly blossoms of your future.

Turn to that page where your eyes speak as one
with the visions of glorious eternity. Know yourself
fearlessly (even quietly) for all the things you are.
Each star is a mirror reflecting the truth inside you.
Every roaring sigh of the ocean a mystic remembering
   God's name.

"Botanical Gardens #2"
(after a painting by Luther E. Vann)

In the presence of beauty the soul
demands that one becomes beautiful.
The craggy shells of our faithlessness
and our coldly churning hunger for death
bursts open like a pod full of promises.

That which is God within us
opens like a thousand blossoms
of purest starlight.
And we see ourselves as if
in the mirror of a true angel's love.

Our chains drift free and dance
naked with our laughter. We float
from this world to the next and back
again, like children learning a game we
taught ourselves a billion years ago.

The Seeker

(after a painting by Luther E. Vann)

Standing sometimes kneeling before
the storms of existence people suffer
things that are ugly and beautiful,
wise and ignorant sad and marvelous

a little girl quietly explodes at the
presence of mystery expanding her womb
a grown man reads the hieroglyphics of
disease within his blood and screams to Jesus

women older than the earth discover
whole galaxies of love hidden in their bosoms
life happens before one knows what it is
time's clues come too few too slow too cold

"enlightenment" tells only half the story
nevertheless the storm that raged becomes
but a single syllable whispered lovingly
to the hearts of those who fought to hear.

The Unseen Companion

This place shall not be warm.
Nor shall you find its cool breath pleasant.
With a heart heavier than death
you will wonder when and how
you came to occupy such a deadly stone.
There shall be no lovely voice begging and weeping
for the company of your sweet tongue.
Despair shall pimp you like a whore
and sell your thighs for less than a dime.
Then a moment, shaped like an angel,
and a time and space as brilliant as a comet,
shall rise above the horizon of your
battered affection, and peace will lift you
like a diamond made out of pure love.
As if stepping from a cloud, one name
shall come forward to embrace your tears.
You will almost know who I am.
In a place secret and safe,
you will almost remember this style.
As we dazzle, and merge, and vibrate like twin
realities flowing back and forth
between our birth and our eternity.
When all the lights fold back into their silence,
in a place secret and safe, warm and fragrant like stars,
you will realize without thought, or sound or color,
that for one second I stood knee-deep inside your heart.
You had gone looking for a friend, and one had found you.

The Drawing of the Two Dervishes

In the drawing of the "Two Dervishes," yours is the robe
with gazelles leaping beyond the snarls of lions,
like wisdom avoiding the excrement teeth of ignorance.
Then trapped by the jaws of the waiting dragon:
like faith, imprisoned, in a world made of lies.

Mine is the robe without color or images, waiting
for your sigh, so rich and heavy with love divine,
to breathe me full of knowledge and form.
Somewhere inside my emptiness time is just beginning.
And somewhere inside my nowhere time has already
  ended.

If you open that book sitting sacred in your hand
out comes an oasis filled with poem-singing birds,
lilac-scented palm trees and moon-dancing waters.
If I open the same book, the earth turns to stone
and every flying thing falls dead upon its face.

I want the existence-and-nonexistence of God to darken
my eyes the way it does yours. Let my tongue dance
the slowdance eloquence of your words' perfect silence.

Song of the Black Skylark

Have you heard the song of the black skylark?
That creature of burning black leaves
found often at midnight on top the gleaming sphere
of Savannah's city hall.
Or sometimes just outside the windows
of those about to die or those being born.

People tell tales, and tales
adorn themselves with legend.
There is one story about a waitress,
she was somebody's mama and daughter,
about 20 or 30, half Muslim, half Jewish,
on her way home walking down Bay street
around 3 a.m. when a manbeast strolled
out of an alley and struck her to the ground.
His thick hands had already torn through
her blouse, and pointed teeth like razors
sliced her skirt and muscular thighs.
A naked rage jutted from his crotch
and dripped hot ignorance all over
the woman's exposed flesh. Just above
the street where they struggled, there in the window
of a second-floor apartment was another
man and woman watching the manbeast
rattle fury all over the screaming waitress.
They watched until overtaken by a heat
that slammed them banging against the windowsill.

And that was when the sound came.

It curved like a screeching arrow
arching up out of the river behind city hall

but at the same time that sound fell,
like a smoking moon shouting out prophecies,
it rolled down the street like a hurricane of jazz singers
and exploded out the sky like a god of love
outraged by the shadow of his own apathy.

The street shook and the manbeast emptied like a pig.
In the middle of their kiss, the couple in the window
erupted nausea from one mouth to the other.

The song of the black skylark blossomed
into a tidal wave of molten earth
that swallowed the manbeast whole
and flooded the window of the blissless couple
like a huge shroud of death stink with horror.
When silence descended over the street
the waitress lay on her back thinking she was dead.
Then slowly her eyes opened. She claimed later
that a large black bird, something other
than crow or a raven, was standing on top
of a man's skull. One arm of the skeleton
pointed up as if in recognition of a vision.
This bird, she said, suddenly flared like a heaven
then shrunk into a silhouette against the full moon.

From that impossible distance she could hear the bird
until the flow of its roar pulled her to her feet
and she looked up again, this time to see two more
skeletons fallen against a window in an apartment
above the street. Like anybody would have done,
she began to run. As she went past city hall
the bird landed on its dome and began singing.

Many people said they both heard and saw it
just as the sun was rising. And the rain that fell

14

from a clear sky that morning, they all claimed,
　　were the tears
of the sun, and that bird, weeping for the dead.

Vampire Song: The Last Bloodfeast

All My lovely vampires went to hell last night.
And the diamond fangs of malice
that so pleasured my throat's whimpering pulse
sparkle bright upon the screaming lawn,
the final gifts of my destroyed lovers' passion.
How did horror strike such a final blow?
And why did misery rape the happiness that was mine?
With fingers too slick with red, eyes too thick
with lust, no one saw the deadly moment approach.

I had sat as always, atop a table of rose quartz —
in the center of a golden platter. Sugared grapes
circled my feet, honeyed almonds, camellias and
roasted fowl were garnish around my thighs and hips.
The time had come to bleed and I shuddered with
exquisite anticipation. With rhythms hidden and delicious
my blood swelled into drops that slid through my pores
and sang welcome to the hunger of the vampires.

It was pride that claimed me when a single tongue
tasted my left calf, and joy when another teased
my neck. Fingers two thousand years old wet themselves
on my ruby-stained belly and trembled wildly
on their way to quivering lips. My throat was already
between two fanged mouths when the stranger appeared.

It was not in my nature to feed upon others.
Only to allow others to feed upon me.
Yet there burned a flame in the veins of this stranger
which stirred even my desire. The vampires all
turned away from me and too eagerly, far too eagerly,
flew beside the stranger's splendid naked form.

He offered himself supremely, the bronze wrists
presented like twin virgins, his throat a gleaming new altar,
his sex a calm crescent moon, the eyes two oceans
filled with the roaring soul of the sun.
Bewilderment froze my brain as I watched: muscle by
muscle, and organ by organ his flesh tore between
   their howls.
Then: the smell of blood gave way to an aroma of light.
Eternity bled rapture and forty-eight vampires
   exploded entrails.

I woke up on the rose quartz table, blinking at sunlight.
Clean blood sang through my veins while around me
the heads and limbs of vampires evaporated into
a yellow nothingness. Damnation was all the beauty
I had ever yearned for. Who had saved me
when I had had no desire to be saved?
Soft upon my right thigh, an oddly-colored kitten
meowed the melodies of angels playing violins.

Road Tune

(from Christmas When Music Almost Killed the World)

Traveler oh traveler
do you know where you've been?
I said traveler sweet traveler
is your life still your friend?

Sunrise and sunsets
ride your back like ghosts.
Lord sunrise and sunsets
they ride your back like ghosts.
Between the bitch of your days
and the curse of your nights
can't hardly even tell
what scares you the most.

Well suppose the Queen of Diamonds
played you dead wrong—
I bet the King of Clubs
won't do you no better.
Beauty inside can die forever
when bleeding just to be strong.
Take a needle and thread
of regret sometime
to sew a shredded soul back together.

Traveler oh traveler
do you know where you've been?
I said traveler, sweet traveler
is your life still your friend?

And Then the Rain God Screamed for Love

I am a sloppy lover
that much I will confess.
My kiss has swollen rivers
into torrents of night
and reduced continents
to bashful stuttering islands.
But my eagerness is sincere
and my passion never arid.
Oh behold sweet darling Earth:
the nine billion silver drops
of my fingertips
poised like a species
of liquid birds
suspended
above the hills
and mountains
and deserts
and valleys
of your lush cosmic beauty—
Waiting for you to say "Yes,"
        to say "Touch,"
        to say "Come inside my love,"
        to say "Annihilate,"
        and "Resurrect,"
        and "Where sweet love are you?"

Recall please the fury
of our innocence:
my shy gaze of melting hurricanes
dissolving
in the landslide
of your breath rushing forth like tigers,

recall, please
my fever dropping from the sky
and filling your belly
with sapphires
and rubies
and mysteries neither revealed nor forsaken.

To what did our tremblings give birth?
To oceans of green
and to air
with a knowledge of itself,
to the very lightning
that severed our coupling
with the sad roar
of its jealousy and hunger.

And what was that like
for you?
Lovely Earth of passion
        nailing Jesus to the cross of mankind's ignorance,
Earth of nations wolfing at each others' throats,
Earth of moonlight and crushed hearts
        and days dizzy with beauty,
what was that like for you
seeing my arms turn
suddenly to ghosts
and watching my face
float backward into
the heat's cruel laughter?
I feared the sun
had murdered you
thus I flooded heaven
with a thousand galaxies
of unrelenting vengeance
until my tears

gathered blessings
to fall once more upon your breasts
so sweet there upon your breasts
how lovely there upon your breasts
and it has been
that way ever since:
me spiraling downward
stormy and luscious inside of you
then snatched back into sorrow
by the sun's bitter teeth.

I am rain and thou art the element of my desires,
spread soft the holy garden,
and with this thunder soothe your weeping fire.

How the Sky God Confessed Love for the Skylark

You are neither a phoenix hatched out of paradise
nor an eagle carved from golden distinction.
Your stature poses oddly between crow-sized and
hawk-like, denying the genus to which you belong.
And poets gazing upon you do not frost their tongues
    with praise.
Your color is irresistible for reasons that are unholy.
Your eyes cast nets that liberate the imprisoned.
Where you command power is from the chair of your song;
your trill annihilates and recreates my heart at will.
Symphonies spill from your wings like genesis
pouring down in torrents from the lips of the sun.
If I am a god of some notable stature, it is only
because your soul has given birth to my love,
your wings revealed to my breath its purpose for being.

II. one river crying and another river laughing

"Fulton Street/The Series"
(after a painting by Luther E. Vann)

"The essence of a multidimensional moment,"
muses Luther out loud.

Brown eyes click like a camera lens.
The soul opens like an aperture.
Instantly we are a nation of spirits
unabashedly naked in front of each other.

Beneath the armor of skin/and/ bone/and/mind
most of our colors are amazingly the same.
I read them as intentions or purposes, the way
a schoolboy might study the Quran or Bible.

Evil is mostly confusion
seeking to evolve itself into Love.
This I learn among many other things.

Then light slides over to another side of
the universe and life becomes "normal again."
One day I must tell Aberjhani about what just
happened, but at present I don't know who he is.

Dead River Blues for Langston

River to river to river—
love and beauty and death
stretching for miles the skin of my heart
from high tide to low.
Thinking about America
and the best way to go.

That morning sun,
he always come up bleeding,
and sweet sugar moon,
she mostly go down screamin'.
Between a woman and the door
and the man beneath the floor
I keep sweatin' bout America
and which way I should go.

Whereas my skin is black
my world is sho' nuff white.
Hand jivin' just to beat the blues
and waiting fast for the night.
It's true I ponder as I wander,
but most times I think I know.
On the road to my taste of heaven
I don't mind travelin' slow.

Love and beauty and death—
river to river to river
lynching these dreams swinging naked in my heart,
screaming for mercy from high tide to low,
I think hard about America
and the best way for me to go.

In Regard to a Poet's Birthday
(a.k.a. "Every Poet's Birthday Poem" for Jahannes)

The years whistle best
in their own unruly meter.

Like flawlessly planned
intentions
not all of their lines
have agreed to rhyme.

Once, inside a net
crusted over with indigo pearls
I caught a thousand crystal echoes
of Gnostics sailing their souls
across an ocean
of overheated eternity
and to this day I funnel
that fire through silvered tongue
and goldplated cells.

Funny how a mountain
can sing like a choir or a
single syllable shock like a baptism.
Gifts of hope washed clean
in a lake of platinum ages.

If life is a birthday cake
let my face be smeared
with its icing of cognac and kindness.
Inside the flickering
of a candle's bright laughter
let me breathe a scent of themes
well-chosen and well loved.

"DarkMagusMilesAhead #7"
(after a painting by Roy LaGrone)

Through the glowing-bronze reeds of Harlem midnight
and the plum-rose bloom of Spanish twilight
African-griot-magus waters the garden
of his neon spirals deep in the valley
of my jazz-consoled hunger and madness.

70 x 7,000 miles we travel the naked truth
of hidden beginnings and guessed-at endings,
African-griot-magus inhaling demons more easily
than I exhale peace of mind or clarity of soul.
African-griot-magus balancing divinity like tornadoes
humming on the tips of three angels' tongues.

Lost inside my third mind I build a planet ruled by
    honeysuckle,
violets, and the shadows of voices bubbling soft joy.
With my seventh mind I hammer a chain of wonders
that hold African-griot-magus to all of his promises.
With my ninth mind I resurrect my first
and dance slow to the music of my soul made new.

80 x 8,000 years we sing the naked story of
blue-boned Harlem midnight and plum-rose Spanish
    twilight.
African-griot-magus horn blowing waves of dotted light
that rise in the east and wander blind through the west.

African-griot-magus, face that is my face, unafraid of
destruction, wailing like Joshua illuminated pages
    for a new creation.

Sweet Brother Beat-Bop Daddy K
(3/12/22-10/21/69)

Which take is this
Sweet Brother Beat-Bop Daddy K?

Listen, kid, the first take
is the only take:
you dig deep like skiddly-wee-doo-boy
then shut your stinkin' face.

Which take is this
Sweet Brother Beat-Bop Daddy K?

You get the one shot baby,
you dig deep or you sink deeper.

I write this life
the way I spurt my soul
in jazz-riff streams
across the condomless page
praying Charlie Parker
will blow for me
a higher range of esthetics
redefining and redesigning
everything I never knew
about God-as-me within this world
and who knows how much
we do not know about Love
or lovelessness? Can you spit it
supremely
through saxophone genius
like dark mystic birds
Coltrane and Charlie?

I place my best feet
upon good green earth
running from one session of hell
in America to another
small-town boy French-Canadian sperm
crossing the goal line
straight into the mine fields
of World War II, my sanity
like a fish with hooks
in both eyes, my hunger
like an engine
gulping highways and speed.

Between poetry
and jack-rabbit orgasms
fired below the belts
of women and men
your moon burned bright
black and blue inside and out
alcohol flipping you foul
like a 3 cent whore
bought and paid for
by mother dear's indulgence.
Ginsberg wore the crown
hammered out of your passion,
Burroughs claimed the throne
carved from your skull,
and Neal never got
what Neal wanted bad
and you maybe yeah you needed much much more.

I place my fingers
        upon these keys
        typing 2,000 dreams per minute
        and naked of spirit

dance forth my cosmic vortex
upon this crucifix called language
I am not so calm as Christ
still I dig his style
In ways infinite and bloodless.

"What can a man do for Love?" moaned Lucien
over your grief-rotted corpse.
He thought the answer complex,
it is simple: a man can & should
do everything for love
neither holds nor poles barred.

I place my body
beside these bodies
protean and afraid and much-like flame
I come to you now
full of my man-self
but tomorrow, perhaps, not so hard
somewhat female in ways
or maybe as child
weeping bids for heaven,
what I most want
is to warm your spirit
with this sun rising wild
inside my spirit.

Holy rarely is as holy does
Sweet Brother Beat-Bop Daddy K,
whether you suck your pain
from the bottle or a body
makes little difference,
it's what you choose to swallow
that grants or denies
the good bliss of Buddha
shouting hallelujah through your veins.

Which take is this
Sweet Brother Beat-Bop Daddy K?

Listen, kid, give me grace
or give me death.
I will not stay here Gerardless
Buddhaless and Neal-gone-too.
My Love speaks every name
under every star shining
yet who suckles my heart
with mouth overflowing
Mexico-city sundown marijuana blues
(Stella, is that you?)
my lover and I stoned equally
on sorrow and each other's tongue.

Holy rarely is as holy does
Sweet Brother Beat-Bop Daddy K,
whether you suck your pain
from the bottle or a body
makes little difference,
it's what you choose to swallow
that grants or denies
the good bliss
of a good Buddha
shouting glory-be-to-God through your veins.

When Giants Wave Goodbye

Giants gently waving goodbye
wink lasting legacies to behold,
and wonder if we understood
the brilliant stories their lives told.

Will we ever get the joke
that race plays on human hearts?
Or by religion and nationality,
remain forever torn apart?

Mr. Parks beneath your "Learning Tree"
much wisdom nourished my soul.
In the click and glitter of your camera,
nobility and beauty did unfold.

Such things have meanings, no doubt,
when titans in parade depart earth's shores:
Octavia Butler, Dana Reeve, Coretta Scott King—
and among the unknown, many thousands more.

Giants gently waving goodbye
wink lasting legacies to behold.
I pray we try to understand
the glorious stories their lives told.

American Widow: Song for Coretta Scott King

Martin you could not of course
but you should have seen it,
the wind turned to frozen thorns
 when your coffin kissed the earth,
they drilled leprous holes in my arms
and the children all said
Mama please don't Mama please—
but Friend where are you?
I have searched the bellies
of stars and storms for your
miraculous voice, I have walked seas
and seas of crippled night to hear
the songs of your touch and...

Friend of Mine when the dirt covered
your coffin crowds fainted
in the streets and up on the hills
of their souls our children sang
"I'm goin' up yonder, I'm goin'
up yonder to be with my Lord, "
but not without me I'd always thought.
Oh my Soul, why did you go
so far without me, but the most
wondrous thing, the kind of wondrous
thing that amazed you most
was the sun gushing blood all over
my bereaved life while the preacher
said such nice true things about
you he must have thought
he'd made them up, I recalled

as he spoke, the early days
when we burned like two summers
in the shade of our hearts, I recalled
days of swimming bare-skinned
in the waters of each others'
freedom-hungry minds and even now
a cloud is coming yonder dripping bones
over my bones it is the kind
of wonder that amazed you most
oh dear good Martin, call me to where
you are please I long to show it to you.

Like It is Us

Down and down the road
we was walkin', rain supposed
to be falling from
the western cloud but
it was mud, sliding down
the sky like some burnt
nigger's blood, Eddy got scared
and wanted to go home, but
he was already in his bones.
You already in yo' bones, said
Martha, so he shut up and leaned
on the crutch of her heart, she
smiled like an African tit
and tried to weave a cloth
of the falling mud, David
laughed, said she wasn't doing
it right, he'd already made
a tuxedo for hisself and we
all admitted he looked as
elegant as the Duke's fingers
and we walked on down
and down and down down down
that road of absolutes, of
irrelativities and other snow-
colored words someone peed into
my brain years ago, down way down
marching marching another century gone
the mud was falling like buckets full of night
it should have been rain
and the sun skipped about
the western cloud, Eddy was scared

the western cloud, Eddy was scared
but it was ok for we each of us
knew the value of building huts
out of blood when necessary.

Eli-Jah

(from Christmas When Music Almost Killed the World)

Eli-Jah,
my brother, my friend,
when will I see you again?
Is your heart
safe in love?
Did your war
finally end?
There's a light
out in heaven.
There's an owl
on the roof.
Mom and dad
dreamed you were dead
but I'm still looking
boy for you.
Yes I'm looking
son for you.

In the tree
where we played
robins now
hatch their eggs.
And I can see you
still falling,
hear the wind
forever calling
begging stop
our foolish fights
for soon we'd
know the fright
of this endless endless screaming

and our laughing
boys' life
would lose
its best meaning.

Who could bear
the things we've seen
flying in
and out of dreams?
How angels gave us
pearls to keep
and sang with us
on diamond streets?

Eli-Jah!
My handsome, my twin
I long to see you again.
Is your heart
safe in love?
Did your war
ever end?
There's a storm
in the mountains.
Here's a cross
painted blue.
Lots of holes
in my shoes
but I'm still looking
boy for you,
yes I'm looking
brother for you.

Did I tell you
your son
keeps calling me dad?

Anything less
spins his mind
cold and sad.
In his eyes
shine pictures
of a long-ago you.
In my head
this cruel
unspeakable truth:
that we battled
and we cursed
and we spilled
each other's blood,
we relished
our taste of hell
and strangled
heaven's love.
People said all the time
we were strange that way.
Gave our smiles
 to the moon
and our tears
to the day.

Every Hour Henceforth

I know blackness as taught by my father:
"You are my joy and my genius," he often said.
I know blackness as taught by my mother:
"Your smile is my robe of honor, your peace my
   earned grace."

Once a year we were pilgrims driving from Atlanta
to Waycross where my brother and sister and I
would walk with our parents' memories through the fields
where they and their parents bled through Georgia
   summers,
just barely better off than slaves who died there.
"They took everything but the best thing,"
   my father moaned.

I know divinity as wept by my mother: "Your eyes
are the windows through which He watches over us."
I know divinity as wept by my father: "Your veins
are the halls of glory where He meditates our fate."

There in the fields of ignominies past, our hands
would link and weld like burning rings of truth.
Passing over ground now fruitless and cracked
my father's foot crushed the skull of an albino serpent's evil,
and my mother's heel the sting of a dark scorpion's
   ignorance.
"They killed everything but one good thing," my mother said.

I know power as sung by my father's soul: "Every single one
cut down left you a legacy of strength on top of strength."
I know power as spun by my mother's faith: "Don't matter if
both arms break, your spirit can still lift a whole nation."

We stop at the gray stone —bigger than I, then—
    marking the place
where my father saw his father fall in the fire of a
merciless hour. We gather round him. His tears storm silent.
Each drop splashes my head with pictures: Black Souls cryin'
all together; Black Souls laughin' all together; Black Souls
    shining bright all as one.

"They ruined everything but the sacred thing,"
    said my father.
"We brought the Love with us and we keepin' it still,"
    said my mother.

"Every hour henceforth we are delivered unto blessed
    triumph."

"We brought the Love with us and we keepin' it still."

42

The Color of Things Unknown

By the golden light of my blackness
I see a woman dead
and reborn many centuries over,
her belly rolls fat
with a soft round infinity
and her breasts stand beautiful
with the secret milk of joy and pain.

Beside her walks a man
with a chest like two thrones
and an ebonwood staff
covered with the stories
of days gone & days to come,
his sex hangs heavy
with the hurricane songs
of creation and destruction.

"I think this child
is going to be a trickster,"
speaks the woman
placing her hand made of lilies
over her belly throbbing with infinity.
"I think this child
is going to be black & white & yellow
and very fond of wars
but very much afraid of Love."

The man pressed his lips
upon the woman's belly
until it glowed like a cloud
filled with diamonds:
"I hope this child is born part angel
with wings made from the grace of God,"

spoke the man,
"I hope this child is a humanspirit
with legs of great wisdom
and arms of true prosperity."

As the woman and man walked
and talked beside each other
the woman painted a dream
upon the sleeping face of a full moon
and they saw inside this vision
all those things they had feared:
the greedy mouths of men overflowing
like canals with the blood of other men,
the serpent tongues of women spitting fire
like bullets of envy and hatred for other women.
They looked upon these things
until tears grew the woman's belly larger
and with a kiss in one hand
and a song in the other, the man released
the goldenblack infinity glowing inside the woman.

I want to tell them: mine is the color
of things unknown and mine
 is the dance of a-new-day-rising-fast.
When I open my mouth to speak these words
they hear the sound of one river crying
and another river laughing. Through their eyes
I see myself squirming brightness in my
father's hands and I shine to let them know:
I am not born to become less than what
I already am. I/AM born to establish more.

A Dancer's Strength and Grace

In the brilliant pages of
"The Women Who Raised Me"
a daughter born to destiny
is what one clearly sees.

Challenged from the start
by the blood of history flooding her path—
crashing waves of denial and shame,
racism screaming its scornful wrath.

Consider her skin the color
of America's dream of democracy;
a ward of the state of Maine, yes,
but a child as well of aristocracy.

Through the schizophrenic shadows
of her mother's pleading tears,
caring hearts sang strong angelic prayers
to guide her through the years.

With a philosopher's taste for wisdom,
and a dancer's strength and grace,
over pits of hell and sorrow she leaps
to run a blessed and noble race.

If Love is a kind of country
where royalty is determined by beauty of soul,
then somewhere waiting for Victoria Rowell
is a glittering crown of diamonds and gold.

All in a Day's Work

This is the work of the body:
to grow ever-mindful of spirit.
Feet sledge-hammer boneflesh
upon a pavement of unforgiving reality
to a rhythm of heel-step-breathe heel-step-pray...

This is the work of the soul:
to honor purposes of mind and body.
Love slides down the side of the heart
like a mud of silk and funk and perfume
rushing down mighty Kilimanjaro.

Muscles stretch from star to moon to heart,
shrink to a single comet; the sweet
heave-ho of flesh awakens to higher intention.
Pain like an over-efficient android
builds metallic agonies of nerve and thought.
Joy like a forty-day flood of acrylic roses.

This is the work of the body/soul.
Breath of perseverance pumps determination
the way engines of eternity spew fresh planets.
Fingers of faith clench a gnarled fist of freedom.
A hook and line dipping deep
into rolling streams of a would-be heaven
snag on the sunken treasure of unexpected grace.

III. supremely robed in the diamonds of his skin and shadows

That Poem is Not My Brother

"...In other words the consciousness
bears witness to its own voice... And
each atom of the universe confesses
by its tone: 'my sole origin is sound.'"
--Hazrat Inayat Khan

The great black blues singer, youngcat that he was,
unhinged his mighty lungs and drew in prana as if he were
the earth herself sucking deep the holy cosmic winds of holy
endless time and preparing to demonstrate for always and
once more the whole sticky thing about eternity, about the
mystery and controversy and the irresistibleness of its beauty.
I looked at Tombstone and he checked me out knowingly
from the corner of an indecipherable gaze then both our
eyes swung with the beat back towards the current world-
order blues master: J.C. Faulkner. He is a much larger—than-
fantasy African cherub who suddenly squatted as if to take
a mountainous shit but who instead unleashed out of his
inner kingdom a laser-cannon blast of hoo-doo hollers and
dead-souls-calling-for-their-rights, his perilous voice ruling
now all life just like the cruciality of a broken heart
commanding one's education. His nose-antenna quivered,
and the song he'd been singing, "Might As Well Be A Dead
Man Blues", came like an electrocuted life to its hot
sputtering end.

First the crowd faded into an astonishment of silence then

49

several chairs and a table too hit the floor as everyone's collective dumbfoundedness boomed with applause that fell like walls then stood up as if tidal waves offering genuine love and the great blues singer stepped back from testifying Gullah Man to born-again college boy, grinning through tortoise-shell spectacles at the noise he'd made the crowd make, letting himself feel along the curves of his more-than-small belly some of the affection drizzling light all around him.

"C'mon, let's say hello to J.C. real quick before we take off."

This suggestion, I swear, is not a surprise to Tombstone who with enviable skill when he responds raises his left eyebrow only. "We can't get anywhere near J.C. You know how his fans like to press and giggle all over him so they feel like they're the star instead of him." Thus spoke Tombstone, so named when caught dickydallying with two lovely femmes atop the tomb of a famous soldier of the War of Northern Agression.

As true or not true as his words were, we probably could'a got to him if we'd been moving instead of talking since our table was second from the front, on the circle outside the circle next to the circle where J.C. had been singing, but by the time we stood it was just as Tombstone self-fulfillingly prophesized: our great bluescat was surrounded by babes and honeys and would-be dudes teething (as in smiling) appreciation and talking much smuckadoody. Even so, as we approached the door and some lonely-heart hand stole a squeeze on my lonely-heart zipper that great angel of midnight tears and unspecified fornications yelled loud my name:

"Hey, Bobby True!"

I turned, and there they were, large eyes shining amber radiance above the heads of the surrounding boy cubs & girl cubs, they poured out that part of his music he never gives completely and which the joy hiding inside never stops singing.

"You brought my song with you, right!?"

50

"Brother you know I did. It's all typed up in my heart but we still dealing with some of that editing and transcribing blues. Know what I mean?"

"Baby if you mean it's not written down yet, that's bullshit! You done gave everybody some damn music except my black and blues singing ass so I need to know what's up with that! Brother?!"

I smile at the way we holler through the crowd, as if we are our ancestors shouting encouragement across rows of cotton and thrilling ourselves with the heedlessness of our mandatory and desperate ignorance. I dig inside the croaker sack shoulder bag snuggled against my left side and ignore the large anonymous palm that casually measures my ass then I pull from the sack a single sheet of paper with lyrics typed black on both white sides, a song I've written, as blues dude J.C. stated, for someone else, But now I fold it into a paper jet and send it zooming through the haze of smoke, thick smell of beer and loud chatter of bar-people towards J,C.'s wiggling reaching fingers.

"Ha ha ha, yeahhh baby! I knew you had some good shit for me. Y'all comin' back for the second set, right?"

These words spoken even before he has tasted my offering of fatted-calf lyrics make me love him without regret. Me and Tombstone slide through the crowded doorway like shadows with certain destinies or erections withdrawing from slippery flame, ease out beneath the stars of a cool November Savannah night. The sparkling crispness of the air wraps our bodies in a cocoon of chilled contrast to the overheated club we have just left. It is one of those schizophrenic Savannah nights where the weather cannot decide if it should be mid-autumn, early winter or thinking maybe about spring and the ocean-scented breeze stirs one's sexual curiosities with one long lazy finger after another. The mind sighs defeatedly. I let my head turn slowly to the right and breathe deep as if while living my heroic life someone is taking care to forget themselves and is, instead, carefully tending to my lips, toes, chest, knees, the innocence of my genitals, someone is approaching me from any number of dimensions with love heavy in both their hands. I fall, nearly, into a flow of dreams, when Tombstone knocks my forehead with his and I assume the parade-rest stance of a docile airman.

"You can sleep and dream anyplace, can't you?"

So fucking what?

We are on the corner of N and B Streets in the main vein of the city's famed historic district, where glittering bars, clubs, restaurants and coffee houses sit wedged between monuments to numerous lies, propped up like tye-dye-haired art students sitting on a bus between popes and nuns. Poets, whores, musicians, artists, homeless philosophers, doctors of one -ology or another, schizophrenic hustlers, thieves and children stick to the nightscene like barnacles on the bottom of a sunken ship's ass. The bars and clubs flash names like The Silk & Wool James Dean, Daddy's Gin & Tonic, The Chicken's Funky Mama and Time To Eat Betty. The Friday night crowd flows from block to block and door to door, boys dressed in jeans and shorts and leather jackets sometimes with matching leather skirts or boots; girls dressed in jeans and shorts and leather jackets sometimes with matching leather skirts or boots. A fog of friendly confusion drifts above the pavement like clouds of moth in luminous anti-motion.

A youngman cheerfully dressed in copper-rimmed glasses rolls toward us on skates pushing before him a shopping cart filled with yellow paper bags, written in bold black on each one are the words: "Yellow Paper Bag." He places one in my hand and offers as well to Tombstone, who does not take it but being taller than the youngman stares over his head across the street at an Amazon womanchild lurching slowdrunk towards us.

"This looks amazingly like a yellow bag, right?" says the young mad-scholar-maybe-scientist-spiritual-little-boy-or-somethin, "This looks like a yellow bag but it's really a key. It's a powerful key to whatever door you need to open. Now

52

some people have found that difficult to believe but I can tell two culture studs like you are among those with eyes that see and ears that hear so you recognize the strength of what I'm offering. We're looking at power on top of power. If you're financially constipated, this yellow bag will unplug you. If you're breath smells like shit, this bag will make it like sunflowers. If impotence is keeping you down instead of up, this bag will give you a hard-on two inches bigger than any you've ever had before. Come on good brothers, you know you recognize a blessing when you see it. Take this bag and prosper."

Warily and excited too one should note I looked Inside the yellow bag but also glanced over at the curvaceous stupor of the youngwoman crossing the street zagging and zigging ever closer toward us. The bag was filled with torn corners and whole pages of nearly every book on that dude's list of titles from what he called his Western Canon or Nordic Slingshot one or the other and I was rather happy staring down into that mass of magnificent brains on paper leaves of knowledge shining up at my mind as if signaling something meaningful, unexpected, true.

Just as I withdrew my head from the bag of the glory of shredded wisdom, the Amazon womanchild stumbled onto the curb, her unambiguous she-ness dressed in black heels, black leather pants and matching interesting leather bra with small circles of chrome looping in and out of her Amazon womanchild face. Drunk and slow: translating as hot and possible. She seemed to me preparing to smile when her belly rippled forward then up and as I held out the yellow bag of timeless intellect her head went inside and spewed forth from Amazonian guts most of the fun she'd been having all night. We left her holding it and the mad-scholar-boy staring disappointedly but lust-burdened too I thought at her twitching puking shape. If there'd been snow and all of us wearing mittens it could have been a scene for a Christmas card but weatherwise it was not cold and fluttering all around us were impulses to be naked of not clothing only but dirty tattered fears and oversized smallnesses.

We walked south half a block to the entrance of an alley nicknamed The Outhouse.

"So what should we do? Go to the Chicken's Funky Mama or walk over to the Gallery Espresso? Receding Wave's doing their poetry gig with an open mic at the Gallery and we might just wanna read a few pieces." This came out of Tombstone a question but in reality stated confirmation cause we'd previously spoken before about these possibilities and said already we were going to the Chicken's Funky Mama but couldn't now and I said why.

"Sherry's band's playing there tonight and I Just gave J.C. the song I, um, kind'a promised to give her."

"I thought she paid you to write that song. Didn't she give you something like a hundred dollars plus some fringe bedroom benefits!?"

"Well, um, in a way, but——"

"That's fucked up Bro'. That's like me accepting advance payment from Time Magazine for a photo shoot then giving the pictures to Newsweek. I mean I understand it's one of those 'black thangs' when it comes to you and J.C. but business IS business, you know?"

"Exactly. That SHOULD be respected too. But J.C. gets the short end of too many sticks man. Equal opportunity is still struggling to get beyond the theoretical stage in this town. And it's not always a black and white issue. Billie Holiday was talkin' to her Mama when she said 'God bless the child that's got his own.'"

"So that means what? You're a self-appointed committee to right the wrongs done to all Brothers?"

"It means I've been promising J.C. songs for a long time so I gave him one. Miz Sherry'll get hers. It just won't be tonight."

At the mouth of the alley called The Outhouse we stood for dramatic long slow moments staring down into the dark-dim midnight-blueness of it all where covered lights one or two at most maybe four stuck like knobby little ghosts to walls above thick heavy doors and despite the whiz-whiz rushing of traffic sneezing behind us we could hear the unbolted throbbings of. . .well: music. blues music, reggae music, world fusion, rock, jazz, country, gospel, folk, new dimensional, techno— music. Squeezing amplified through ancient iron doors and blending to fill the alley with a soft fuzzy cloud of hummmmm. Not wholly unlike famous monks chanting holy.

Even without ever having rehearsed it or giving each other clues signals commands or any similar such things we simultaneously stepped onto the tiny pissy tongue of the alley, each man with his left foot leading boldly where his right foot dared follow. And the poet breathing through my tragic human fingers and paps and feet imagined us as astro-sailors having just stepped from another planet onto the alley-covered plains of Earth, strangers in a land ripe for the taking.

We waded like characters carved out of cool itself into the silk-humming dark of that cement canyon, unmindful of tales of life-taking, sex-snatching, drugscapades and numerous other human misadventures that had given this nonplace its name: The Outhouse.

When we heard the sound, we thought at first one of the bands playing behind the many back entrances had lifted off into overdrive, chronicling by way of sun-eclipsing guitars and soul-fueling drums our every secret intimacy and equally public indiscretions, our claims to disgrace and refusals of nobility. The music we were hearing, we thought, was human-made, but then knew it wasn't. Neither screams nor screeches nor sighs. Was such a vibration possible in this universe, it came odd-curiously like thunder sandwiched between the horrendous and the sublime. Call it the equivalent of an eye speaking in a windless hurricane and what struck our upturned heads as even more dis-believable was the feathered blackness, a winged thing slightly larger than my size-13-regular foot, soaring toward us, wearing its four dimensions of soul-wailing-hot like a cape made of flags from planets known and un-.

Or, as Tombstone later would testify: "We were walking down Outhouse alley when this bird or—it might'a been a big bat—came flying at us making these... weird sounds man. . .sounds like ugly noisy and gorgeous pictures in my head! It shot through the alley like a black laser, then it was gone."

What had we seen? Fearful to know or think or talk about such a mystical-laden thing how it winked at us as if it were a winged lion singing opera In a Disney movie then went away for good or maybe for bad. With the fading of the sound our heads lowered. Tombstone closed his mouth and calmly lit a pre-rolled serving of anesthesia, a gesture more appropriate to me than of him. He bowed his head, praying briefly, then drew his smoke deep, bottling it as if It were the spirit of a lover then held it towards me, but I did not want my derangement compromised any further so smiled and declined. He understood.

We continued walking, little clouds of would-be paradise clinging to Tombstone's black eyebrows, faded rose lips and hair of soft braided antennas pulled into a ponytail trailing messages down his back. His face glowed soft blue electricity as if from visions within and I felt almost that walking beside me was not him but a beautiful flawed idea which someone maybe had had of him. Imagination for a moment displayed a mirror floating before us reflecting our nearly equal heights just over six feet,
my solid broadness and his more sleek branches of sinew, the rich sepia of my African-Americaness and the rose-gold mystery of his Native-American plus Jewish or Irish or black-too-maybe origins. For what they were worth then and there: our origins, in the overcrowded stinkness and the too-lonely beauty of a season prone to suicide and screams confusing themselves with hilarity.

All up and down the alley we passed as we walked twitching globs of life, some of it two dogs fucking with a third whimpering for his turn, some of it not breathing, some of it leaning with back against the alley wall while a face melts between two roman pillars of human thighs, some of it heating up dinner with a spoon and torch, some of it snoring Inside a dumpster dreaming of an island covered with palm trees and lilies.

"Hey, wait a minute Bobby True! Isn't that your brother?!"

My head was turned southwest towards the melting face between big round thighs when Tombstone spoke and I bumped into him where he had stopped.

"Well I didn't wanna say it Tombstone man, but yeah, I think you're right, I think that is your wife. I mean your ex-wife. I think that is Geena."

"What? Geena? What're you talking about? That's a dude! Look. Right there on the ground in front of us. That's your brother Julius."

Like a wheel dreaming of turning, my head rotated east and I looked down. Julius? Stuck like a deceased condom to the alley asphalt? The prodigal one never returned except to steal stereos, love, or food stamps? Stepping directly beside Tombstone I let my gaze crawl a few feet ahead of us to where a single silver-white street light shined down a glittering cone onto the littered asphalt. Within the circle of light white-chalk scribblings on asphalt black glowed like neon hieroglyphics waiting for someone arrogant/ignorant in equal parts to claim she/he understood their every possible meaning. The writings contained a warmth maybe fragrance that drew me to look closer until I stepped to the very edge of the circle of the light then walked with my shadow around the luminous cone from one side to the other. Looking from the opposite side of the shimmering circle the white-chalk hieroglyphics became ordinary English alphabets blocked off into ordinary English words stretched into lines stacked on top of each other to construct what I recognized slowly as—a poem:

"seized by the perils of a resurrection gone wild

I have lost count of my colors and genders
kidnapped by a fuck that never stops
my tongue explodes into thorns
and my chest glows geometric with visions."

"Why'd you call that poem Julius, Tombstone?" I watched as he knelt down and touched several fingers to a couple of the words. "That's just a poem somebody wrote on the ground. Not a very good poem but worthwhile since somebody dug deep enough to find it. You're not erasing it, are you?"

The way Tombstone's mouth sat open pink and brown like a rained-on orchid told me he equally desired one of two things: either to piss the words of f the pavement or cut them into his chest. He stood up while pointing down and barely held back from shouting:

"Did you just say what I think I heard you just say? You stood there and recited poetry while your brother's unconscious at your feet with vomit—or whatever the hell that is—on his face, looking like he's dead or dying or—fuck! Any-damn-thing man! Any-damn-thing!"

The Image of his anguish-bright face flushed fury through my skull.

"How much anesthesia did you smoke tonight?"

The evil incredulity that squeezed his face into a mass of sad wrinkles would have scared me some other time but in this instance served only to stir the embers of smoldering awe. What shook me hard enough to make me wonder if I was hiding some lethal truth from myself was the undisguised unyielding bewilderment screaming out of Tombstone's eyes. Slowed by doubt, I bent down and stretched out my fingers, feeling the black pavement with words written in white chalk until some of it dusted my fingertips. Then I stood, held up my hand to show Tombstone.

"See what's on my hand dude? Chalk!"

"Chalk!? Chalk!? What the hell's wrong with you?! You're standing there with your brother's blood on your hand talking about chalk!? Look, I know you got this trip about dealing with real-life situations like they're dreams, or parables or something, but right now is the wrong time for that. You need to focus in real-time on this real-life serious situation."

"What I SOMETIMES do is interpret life events metaphysically. That doesn't mean I avoid reality, it means I engage it in a specific way. And as poisonous as my brother Julius is, I wouldn't ignore him if he really needed my help. The big question at this moment is how to clear all that smoke out'a your brain so you can stop confusing this poem on the ground with a sentient being."

"Damn, am I hearing this for real? Ok. Cool. This isn't Julius on the ground. It's a poem. I'm now going to pick this poem up, carry it to the car and take it to a hospital."

"And why would you do that Tombstone?"

"Because this poem is hurt Bobby True and it needs a medical editor very badly."

He should have known what he proposed would be impossible. The moment he lifted the poem into his arms, letters and whole words went rolling all over the alley. I marveled at the sight of an "0" bouncing off the wall and an "X" getting stuck between two bricks. As he struggled to embrace a non-existent body, Tombstone's arms crossed themselves and he held his torso like a man desperate to share a hug.

"Hey this is your brother I'm carrying man! Shit, help me!"

His hands flailing among the scattering alphabets made me think of seagulls dipping in and out of ocean surf. A small and precise laser of pain entered my right temple and splintered, thin beams of agony ricocheting from one point to another inside my face and I admitted to my sorrow that the words and letters swamping all around Tombstone were somewhat somehow somehow just as wrong as his claim that my brother was in that alley somewhere. But how to know such a thing for sure is: difficult. Difficult. He kept speaking Julius' name, a talisman of echoes that wasted no time choking him hoarse. A talisman: a thing around the neck like the boy-now-man became a thing around the neck always his needles and bottles and dis-eases offered childlike in exchange for one's own destruction. Julius. His months and years of jail-time offered before the snuffed out candle of faith-in-anything-at-all, his atrophied adulthood exchanged for a favored side of the bed, his blood and vomit on an alley floor testifying to whose inability to save him from brutal self?

Julius when last we met you had peed in your pants, a good thing you said for the smell woke you up to newer possibilities in your present lifetime and you spoke of returning to school for a diploma of some sort, you said you loved your sons and one day would day would figure out what that means, you got drunk and kissed my forehead while swearing on Mama's grave that God is good then you hit me with an empty gin bottle and took thirty dollars out of my wallet. I suspect my head is bleeding at this very moment.

Somehow Tombstone gathered the wobbly words of the poem into his arms so that the long heavy hiss of lines lay draped across his forearms as if they had died suddenly for our sins. In the doorway of our ten years of familiarity we each faced our history of explaining one another's inner-terrain lengthy and involved and he knew whatever load he'd taken into his arms he was going to carry alone. I considered crying. I considered kissing the palms of his hands. I decided not to suppress a fart. I moved two steps forward, my gaze slowly unhinging all sense of obligation to sadness or elation. And behind me with his arms full of weighty words, Tombstone moved slowly, his feet dragging noise alongside their posed compassion. Where were we going, following each other by ignoring each other?
We had nearly reached the alley's end when either the smell of someone sighing or a whisper of wings rolled off of

the south wall. No one stood In front of me yet I felt the coolness of an adult hand reach inside my shirt, gently caress the left side of my ribs and tilt my torso until I looked towards the north wall.

Standing there was a creature of such intense nonreality and beauty that he could have been any number of illusions, a ghost or fallen constellation for example, or a blossoming jasmine suddenly made flesh, but mostly he looked like a man staring upward at information floating down from the sky. He stood with shoulders and one foot propped against the back door to one of the clubs—the Silk & Wool James Dean I think—and the feeling was that he'd been born there fully grown six-and-a-half feet tall and dressed just the way be was, in uncovered skin and color flowing between bronze and cinnamon. Face of African lines richly sculptured, his head tilted back with eyes arrowed skyward seemingly seeing people praying just beyond the nonvisible moon, his hair a vibrating mass of afro tangled with stray dreads and locks of ebony like feathers and knives, the whole structure of his muscles linking with a harmony nonchalant and also ethereal. A light against his throat sparkled like expensive jewels and wine-liquid spells flowed out of him as wordless songs with the same ease that honeybirds illuminate myth. To say it simple the feeling was that he was not standing there naked in an alley humming bits of magic but that bits of magic were very masterfully humming and improvising naked him.

Memory of moving toward that creature escapes me. I recall only time fainting and collapsing and my head resting with sudden desperation on top of his bare huge foot then Tombstone yelling at me for long other-dimensional minutes until I did cry this time and levitated to a standing position then walked back to where the cup of Tombstone's arms overflowed gallons of undiluted torture. Shame slid its tongue inside my mouth and my heart turned away from my mind's endless begging. Against the wall that beautiful entity never looked at us but kept his gaze circling frequencies flashing far above our heads.

Tombstone like me was quiet now, his shoulder and back still bent forward as if the weight of his imaginings truly was my brother's body bleeding all over his life or as if the poem in his arms contained within it the secret unbearable substance of every person's glory and agony. My silence glanced long and boldly in a save-me-please kind of way at the black-being so supremely robed in the diamonds of his skin and shadows and chants. Several blocks to the north a tugboat struggling down the Savannah River bellowed against the night like a beached whale suffering unnatural acts at the hands of humans. We stepped like ragged walking rage out of Outhouse Alley and my bones jumped with fear, thinking for a moment I'd heard the universe screaming for my head.

IV. that's how we ebony skylarks are

My Soul Lighting Candles

Did a blue and black skylark
build its nest lined with pearls
in the ruby-leaved branches of your heart?

Did he shake his feathers
like a lover naked in paradise
and scatter black diamonds through the fields of your soul?

Some days I fly east, some days west,
my song tumbling along the breeze
of God's lightest chuckle.

Through clouds. Now sun. Now rainbows and stars.

My soul lighting candles
upon the sapphire moons of your breasts
clears the path love glides all over this broken-hearted
world.

I've been told a sacred melody
spun your flesh into thread
and wove your tears into a carpet made for praying.

That's how we ebony skylarks are—
singing dreamers up out of their sleep
and dancing the dead away from their graves.

Delightful Aesthetics of Divine Dreamers

And I dreamed you were painting me
dreaming of painting you
watching yourself spin fire into a woman
made of orchid wine and nylon roses.

Look at how your lips re-shape with song,
and joy, the aesthetics of my desire.

The smoky sweetness of your spirit
curled up from the mink thatch
of your heat and splattered the canvas
of love's untamed genius.
I drew you deep inside every cell—
exhaled tenderly the sacred kiss of us.

See the way our souls vibrate bright heavens
shooting naked through our hearts.

In a bombed-out Moroccan market
your eyes laughed the riddles
and your tongue wept the parables
that cradle this planet's lonely faith.
Almost: I learned something about divine design.
About the warm holiness that makes it credible.

Listen to how we sigh soaked in all these colors.

As I slid and burned skin with you
through reflections of fantasies
stepping boldly into flesh—

I nearly learned something about love.
About the way it dreams of us,
dreaming lives and worlds for each other.

Blue Madonna Rising

Mother of spirits, of music-babes
dreamed pure as breath of secret dawns,
your flesh-eyes are the spinning lights
of Gemini. And your far-seeing third eye
the whispering planet of Venus.
With hips like Africa's rocking cradle

and breasts like sun-ripened roses
you lie dreaming in the desert,
the diamond-cleansed milk of your soul
giving strength to infant voices,
the star-nourished fruit of your visions
squeezing overripe poems out of ancient prayers.

In my ring of kef I step back
to cold Christmas mornings when heat shed my flesh
to rhythms of my love for you.

We danced a cosmic dance wild and divine
and you were the song I always sang best.
I was the spell of burning tongues
you most loved to cast—
the sweet and the sweet, you and I,
slowly seducing time's fascination with itself.

Almost immaculate. Almost angels.
Within our blessed embrace
Love giggled and shined tirelessly,
always eager
to give her perfectly flawed self
to her other perfectly flawed self.

Spiral Flower Ascending

Odd like waves of silvergold twilight
the roots of your ancient hunger
spread through the sensuous belly of this earth
surge and stretch like underground lightning
nibbling the fruit of a joyful delight.

Everything you taste is only half of what I am.

The stem and bud of your purpose and need
breaks the drought-hardened surface
like an over-thirsty young lover
licking at honey on an angry bear's paw,
naked as a raindrop and green as good fortune
beneath the curious adoration of the sun
you travel circles of gold inside circles of gold
your jade leaves and pregnant petals
like the breasts of Venus shaking tambourines
till thunder weeps wild his wild and dreamy ballad.

Through my mouth light flows reflections of your soul dressed
in painted skins.

Around this world and above it from
Jupiter to Andromeda to the garden in your eyes
you sail love's blossoms all over this universe
each one delivers the infant of a new star
rising as you shine, shining as you rise
Spiral Flower trembling a cool hot breeze against the dawn
of her ascension.

A black skylark rolls time on his tongue
singing rivers of angels to carry her through.

KOO 4

A dream full of flame-devouring eagles.
This is the way of the sky deep inside God's hand.
Neither sleep nor prayers come here.
Only trembling tears. Your lips. This gentle deadly light.

The View from Where We Love

I noticed it climbing up—
each blade of grass
burned smooth lips of light
with their own private hue,
all flip sides of jade—
the secret passions of violet,
the erotic invitations of red.
Tucked in the mountain's sides were
several boulders made from
that solid light born
of a single shared kiss.
A cave flooded
with thousands of chanting fireflies
glowing your world inside out.

At the bottom
I had started in stone boots
and forty-pound furs.
Half-way up, a pink wind
warm as an unborn spirit
pressed me teasingly
against a silver tree
of knowledge divine
and shredded from my limbs
the weight and skin of dead beasts.
Wrapped my knees and genitals,
my chest and face
in the cloak of a healing sigh.

Reaching the top
my stone boots crumbled
and I sat with crossed legs

upon a carpet of painted fire,
rainbows pouring through my hands
like sweet wounds of grace
bleeding a naked peace
for all this world to see.

From the raw edge of the summit

I looked out on the sea—
a mahogany ship with giant sails
shaped and colored
like eyes born wide open in Egypt
dreamed of the history of the future.
In the waves beside its hull
floated a rose longer than a whale.
And the rising sun showered gold
upon a cloud of pearl-blue angels.
A dolphin leapt high to kiss
a jewel-titted humming bird.

Within a song-filled field behind the sky
a woman made of joy
danced naked to the sizzling music
of a winged candle of hope.
I sat in love's fire watching
eagles of lightning lift and scream
your soul out of my chest
and wing their way toward the jubilant dawn.

KOO 2

Sheets of night unwind
like silk from about my head.
Jupiter pumps us full of giddiness.
The moon, stars, the wind
splash like lovers
in the sizzling lake of this kiss.

Up on Passion's Rooftop

You sneezed like a drunken trombone
shouting loud Creator's name
and my heart, my poor foolish
kite-flying tambourine of a heart
thought you were singing sonnets.
So I danced. On our mattress.
Until the bed splintered
like wood for kindling Gnostic joy.

You turned emerald inside a dream
and your hair smiled across my face
like a perfumed sonata
sprinkling piano dust over the ocean.
Thus I woke and screamed, "Look!
Look! Winter at last is dead and gone!"

Naked I ran through moonfire
and broke frozen ground
that I might sow seeds of fleshy bliss
and watch them blossom tributes
to the lyrical rose of your beauty.
Naked I nibbled your thorns to their quaking core.

But what is this sweet annihilation
of all sense and sensibility
each time love flies through the door
of my heart's mud-and-stick palace?
What is this slow blue dream of living,
and this fevered death by dreaming?

You begged me to tell you where
day hides night, and night hides you.

Are mine the lips to say dear poet?

I am just a broken-headed lion
stalking game up on passion's rooftop,
roaring teeth at the moon that once was my mind,
exploding bones at the scent of stars weeping wine.

Abstractions of a Passion Divine
(song for a spiral flower in her season)

Inquisitive woman.

Dream-lovely black woman.

Woman with my soul
glowing naked inside her heart.

Songs and tears overflow
the midnight secret
of our lips butterflying magic
each praying spells to save the other
from the hissing stones
of a southern desert piled high
with smoking skulls and shattered spirits.

Ancient black love.

A morning soaked wet with storms.

Twilight blowing warm between petals of jazz and magnolia.

The divine black voice
of a holy blues man
wraps us shameless inside
the tattooed halo of our angelic madness.

Who am I to say
"hush little baby...hush"

with the moon sobbing gardens of bliss upon the ebony
chest of the night?

How can I command
"don't you cry"

with all these stars weeping crystal roses at your beautiful
brown feet?

Coffee Morning Rhapsody

The feeling is that I have grown a second pair of eyes.
Behind or within the brown ones looking out at you.
A third ear and multiple improvisations beating through
   my heart.
This is my life sitting across from you
raptured in aromas of coffee schooled in Kenya,
the silk music of our nudity and the air of our modern ways
perched like sparrows chirping over the world's
   glass-rimmed edge.

This brew is heady and the danger soothing as our nostrils
fill with the same bliss that kindling sex
has established upon this cool and fragile morning.

Stars breathe themselves to life inside your hair and laughter
as I watch the evolutions of constellations
patterned after our years together. I am reminded
how much of me now lives inside of you.
I see my smile riding the blaze of a comet
traveling a slow ellipse from the sun
and moon of your breasts to the wisdom rising
in the center of your brow and returning to flare again.
When the cup in your hand shakes and your eyes lift
like wings made out of God's prayers: I know
that you have entered my mystery
and found yourself there, and loved yourself there.

Strange to feel this way simply because the sun
is coming and I am swallowing undiluted magic.
When I say that out loud does it sound insane?
If I say your voice is an amber waterfall in which
I yearn to burn each day, if you eat my mouth

like a mystical rose with powers of healing and damnation,
If I confess that your body is the only
civilization I long to experience... would it mean
that we are close to knowing something about love?

Such is my life sitting across from you
raptured in aromas of coffee schooled in Kenya.
This brew is heady and the danger soothing.
   This peace: is fragile.

My One Favorite City

My one favorite city is a kiss shared with you.
Make it on any street corner whatsoever,
above any orphaned moon you might please,
beneath a flag on this planet or another,
so long as the lips are yours and the pleasure ours.

I champion all laws forbidding my life
to wander too far from yours.
And I worship the swirling patterns
of divine satisfaction that adorn
my soul's wretched skyline
each time your breath swallows mine.

Festivals in New York cannot match
the riot-filled crush of our stars pressed together.
In neither Moscow nor Madrid
do the domes gleam with the kind of gold
that your whispers melt inside my heart.

My only favorite city is a kiss shared with you.
Make it on a Tuesday, Wednesday, Friday night
or Monday morning. Otherwise, give me Paris
with your face painted on every window.
Or give me a sidewalk café high up in heaven,
where angels and the light adore you as much as I.

Shadow Candy

A pair of small brown hills wrapped in skin,
growing fat with the beauty of fire.

Your tongue circles my danger
like some cat out of Persia
stealthing around two chained Dobermans.

Our pleasure strokes the air
until it hisses white
and forms an island made of chanting steam.

Every tear that drops from my heart
makes you hungry for another.

I watch the sticky candy our shadows make,
up there, on the ceiling
and feel ashamed because I feel no shame.

Fury sweeter than grapes purple on their vine
takes over our singular heat
like thunder drunk and heavy upon the soft-furred mountain.

It doesn't matter if my eyes are closed or open.
I have been this blind and this lost inside of you for days.

Spinning around and turning over, turning over
and spinning around, begging louder and louder for more.

The Golden Art of Dreaming Naked

1.
The sound of drums strip us nude,
bang heated spells around
a circle of dream-dancers
diving in and out of painted flame,
chanting light from one heart to another.

2.
"What a lover's heart knows
let no man's brain dispute."

3.
Above our heads
twin cyber-moons blink
silver kilobytes of secret pleasures
and naked joy shooting meteorites
across the trembling midnight blue
of our slow red rhythms screaming gold.

4.
"What a lover's soul declares
let no woman's tongue refute."

5.
Together we open a book with pages
made of chocolate. And words
written in warm strawberry cream.
We read aloud and make a mess.
Understanding comes slowly,
sweetly, as we lick it off each other—
this tasty language of poetry and dreams fulfilled.

Teaching Fire How to Burn

What sweet impossibility
did you paint inside my mouth?

What is this taste of you that makes
my tongue blind to all except
the healing spice of your name?

My petals had already fallen,
my leaves withered and gone,
when out of the hills of your soul
rain came laughing like balm,
changing the stony wood of my coffin
into a ship fit for sailing.

Snuggled warm inside
this blanket of your genius and passion,
the goddess inside my heart kneels weeping,
making a fresh fire for the god inside your heart.
Through the window of the flame in her hands
you can almost see who I am.

Every dream I have is soaked in trembling supplication.
My every breath is a dream of you teaching fire
  how to burn.

A Jade Hieroglyphic

The silk-bound book of your journey
fell smoking upon the table of my heart.

Just like that.

The jigsaw puzzle of my yearnings for you
tattooed a jade hieroglyphic upon your breast.

Just like that.

What am I doing
wandering naked through the forest
of your illuminated pages,
blood-wrestling with angels
and shadow-dancing with demons?

Why is your heart nailing portraits of sorrow
against the crystal walls of my soul?

All decked out in the myth of Sheba's beauty
and sporting the crown
of your life's splendid unfoldment
you drink the champagne of creation
like an empress reborn to her throne.

Why is my soul chiseling statues of tears
inside the secret valleys of your smile?

Just like that: blind drunk on the wine of your eyes.

Just like that: torched by the sizzle of love without disguise.

Just like that: an epic and a legend locked inside heaven's
vision.

"SAME-SAME"
(porchocolatberrimichele)

The mind sewing quilts inside my mind
shines prismatic beams
of gold-dust eros and lavender-eve wisdom.

Blossoms a gorgeous new language
in chromatic shades and river-tone songs.
Sweetchocolateberry gender warmer than mine.

This mind fingering mosaics all over my mind
grows wild inside my heart
a garden heavy with the pussywillow breeze
of hummingbirds moaning pure bright love.

Buried alive I am/we are staring at
God's chin resting upon our prayers.

Ships glide through fire: on the oceans of this mind.
Dolphins nibble like poets: upon the sugared breasts
    of lilies.

Pearls and diamonds glitter genius: from one moon
    to another.

This mind knitting flesh to spirit inside my mind sings a
chant divine: "same-same, pretty baby, you me
    same-same, yeah yeah."

Scraping Concrete

Tell me what it looked like
clinging to the goodbye click of your heels
scraping concrete for pieces of my mind.

And the frozen hate you spat.
What did it taste like,
burying my heart beneath a street steaming with shattered
hearts?

The dagger laughing in your hand
looked just like a kiss. Loved the way it shined.
Loved letting my mouth wait.

Without wings, you said,
my beauty flies with the same elegance
as a skylark dressed in black fire.

An old man described it as a broken-boned kite.
A young woman said it smelled like a fireplace
filled with the screams of roses burned alive.

The one I need to hear is you.

Tell me what my soul looked like
clinging to the goodbye click of your heels
scraping concrete for pieces of my mind.

KOO 7

Mountains, angels, oceans—
these blocked my journey to you.

Mountains, angels, oceans—
all saw me safely to your heart.

The Coming of Angels

Having tasted the music of your nakedness
I know the feathers on your back
are small but numerous. Patterned like
a large heart made of snowflakes and lullabies.

Trembling like smoke hiding behind midnight's tongue
I swear you are pure beauty and nothing else,
the holy geometry of your tenderness
wrapping me in spirals of smoldering infinity.

The moment your flame withdrew from my arms
dressed in the ways of uncertain daylight...
I wondered what others would see
measuring your glide from corner to corner.

Who, or what, would they say you are? A rare kind of
blackthug with a psychotic disposition? A dyke suffering
manic depression? A whiteboy hammered by self-delusion?
What would bigotry say about its love for your eyes?

It remains customary in this world: to kill one's neighbors.
To rape fellow human beings, to murder children.
Now that your touch dwells among us what
method shall we choose to welcome angels in flight?

KOO 6

Once I knew every definition
of each one of my selves.
Then your voice, like a garden,
revealed three million secrets. About that.
Now I know only this path leading
to the jeweled gates of your laughter.

A Light of Sacred Whispers

The moon waking upon the shore
of your sable-coated breasts
shined upon me
a light of sacred whispers
saying "Thou and I have never been
'Thou and I' – we were born
and evolve as one."

Searching for a mind long lost
I found it shaping colors
and history near the cliffs of your heart.
In my knee-torn jeans
and dirty white cap I stood swaying
beneath the symphony
of your alchemical perfumes.

Egyptian woman flown out of eternity
come to heal my bleeding
with the crushed stars of your tears
and the melted rose of your tongue,
my soul glides like prayers through
the rhapsody of your song on fire.

My voice in your throat
danced to the thunder
of one revelation face to face with another --

      The music in your eyes: my understanding of
          God's joy.

      The incense in your kiss: my understanding of
          God's passion.

The seven worlds of your soul: my celebration
of God's Love.

The sun dreaming above the garden
of your angel-feathered eyes
burned into my gaze
a spell for hungry lovers
saying "Thou & I
whether apart or together
we were created and we remain as one."

Gratitudes of a Dozen Roses

I.
This rose of spiritual gratitude placed at the feet
of a Rasta Warrior Woman showers the earth
with sweetfire and hosannas and early morning glory.

II.
Beneath an African moon shining silver poems
and a river of orchards singing purple praises a black rose
bows her head like a black swan humbled by her crown of
jade.

III.
Birdsongs weave grace in southern midnight like
wine-drunk fireflies. Inside this music of earthly spheres
a bronze rose pulses unspeakable peace.

IV.
For the sake of a mountain where heaven smiles at heaven,
for the sake of streams rushing sonatas toward the future:
a dew-covered delight shakes crystal secrets from her red
velvet bosom.

V.
Crawling sleepily out of dreams tendered
upon pink petals of quiet ecstasy everlasting and everlasting
an island-flavored perfume echoes the scent of a rose.

VI.
Roots of a new beginning spread piously forward
into vines of passion and leaves of revelation,
healing petals from the thorny joy of an angel called Jah
Gabriel.

VII.
A blossom like the naked mystical eye of truth.
Leaves like hands praying down thunder and burning and
rain.
Stem like the backbone of a good strong heart.

VIII.
What is more powerful than the killing crucifixion
of desert heat commanded by a sun with no mercy?
The perfect shade of a flawless rose afloat above the earth.

IX.
With its leaves so rich and heavy with elation
and its crimson face made brighter with visions of divinity
the shadow of a certain rose looks just like an angel eating
light.

X.
The thorn is a bridge spanning the muddy depths
of agony and sorrow so that one may on the other
side dance to the drums of the rose of joy.

XI.
This rose of pearl-coated infinity transforms
the diseased slums of a broken heart
into a palace made of psalms and gold.

XII.
And this one is of eternity. It never stops opening.
The beauty it shines is the same as the path it travels in and
out
of paradise, every second, of every hour, of every day that
comes and goes.

V. where echoes of heaven sighed peace

Holiday Letter for a Poet Gone to War

If in the midst of mannequin bombs
disemboweling pregnant insanity,
a poem of love should seduce your lips,
sing each soul-dazzling stanza
with such soft rapture as an angel might.

If your comrade's head should explode while
you sing with such soft rapture as an angel might,
bandage your heart with thoughts of simpler things—
mowing the lawn, washing dishes,
waking up dreaming in your lover's arms.

What can bombs know of the illuminated fields
so golden with heaven in your heart's sacred lands?
How can bullets hope to penetrate the armor
of your soul's endless capacity for love?

If death should suck the marrow from your bones
while you mow the lawn, wash dishes,
or wake up dreaming in your lover's arms,
remember: you were born a child of light's wonderful
    secret—
you return to the beauty you have always been.

An Angel for New Orleans

O' echoes of marching saints
drum loud your songs of healing.

The improvised wings
of your feathered blue notes and neon blood
spread wide now
like the sacred myth
and swaggering hips
of your heart pulsing reserves of strength
through traumatized veins.

Holy jazzmen of small mystic hours
blow ye furious the rainbow of hope.

French Quarter of elegant mystique, Monica Blache,
Canal Street, Gustave Brother to My Visions,
Super Dome battered humble,
Jerry Bolton and Mississippi and Alabama,
beloved kins-people of Nordette Adams,
abused children all of the wind-goddess Katrina,
from our souls to your spirits
a halo like a world to embrace your trembling.

Sons and daughters of the Christ fire burning,
burn a perfect peace precisely where you are.

O' Tap-dance Kings of Better Days,
O' Gospel Queens of Prophetic Ways,
Princes of Tears and Princesses of Prayers,
feel these weeping arms lifting your arms,
feel these raging hearts beating within your hearts,
welcome this hope-filled breath to increase your breath,

feel these determined legs carrying your legs.

Scent and shadow of a bitch's brew fade like lies rescinded.
Light of angelic eyes shine faith, speak compassion,
   bring love.

A Blue Rose for the Sergeant

The seed that grew this rose
formed long ago.
It was something like a pearl
that fell from God's loving eyes
and planted itself deep inside
the mysteries of this chaotic world.

The roots made their own space
and spread out through love shared
between people common to our lives:
your son Moses and my sister Vera.

Blessed by angelic silence
and nurtured by ancient wisdom
the seedling stem of this sky blue rose
broke through dirt and concrete
like a revelation foretold
breaking through the ignorance
of those too blind to see
and those too afraid to hear.

Then came the pain of thorns
produced from bitter experience.
And the unfoldment of elegant green leaves
developed out of secret knowledge
and the clear spiritual vision
of a humble dreaming prophet.

That we are able to honor
and share with one another

the bright pieces of heaven inside us
is what makes the rose
of this sacred kinship blossom all year round.
It is what anoints our lives in a holy way
with this rose oil perfume
of sweet grace, good faith, and enduring love.

Louie the Madman Cries For the World

Hey you there! You boy! Yeah you, come here!
Hell, I know you 48 years old but a man
ain't nothin' but a size extra-large boy pretendin'
he know why he wake up stinkin' and coughin' and
fornicatin' every day. So shut up and listen.
Boy I been watchin' you for some weeks now,
Drivin' that po' pitiful wreck back an' forth
to a job barely pay you 90 cents a day,
then goin' home to that seven-foot woman
beatin' on your butt like Ali hungry for his comeback.
It's true boy, I sho nuff been watchin' you sittin' on
the toilet bowl of life, dreaming all the things some
nice hot prune juice could do for your constipated
   dispossession.
Singing your Lysol blues till they turn all funky red.

Well, boy, I want you to know:
I'm here to cry for your wretched behind
cause chances are nobody else gon give a shit.
So here, take this first tear for that time
you told your daddy you loved him and he
didn't have a clue who you or your mama was.
This second tear is for when you stopped this morning
to smell some roses and three seagulls stopped to
wipe their rumps on your head. Damn nasty
   feathered heathens.

But we can't cry just for ourselves, so this next batch
of tears is for the amputated refugees of Sierra Leone

and the genocide children of Rwanda and Somalia,
   yes, and no,
for the raped flesh of the earth and the prostituted
   genius of poets,
O' for the sorrows and horrors of this world I slam
the drums of my blood and who dares dance with me!?
For the power-drunk tyrants and junkie-fevered
bombers, for the drowned prophets of Haiti and the
slaughtered humbles of Asia I weep a crimson
   tsunami of exploded hearts.
O' for the shame and pain of this life I belch the nails
of my tormented soul and who dares howl with me!?

Damn, boy, this crying for the world can wear your ass out.

Did I tell you I fell asleep under a bridge for 20 years
and while I dreamed people used and abused me bad?
Still I got a head like a hammer and a heart like the moon.
All kinds 'a things we could cry for in this world
but then I noticed that same seven-foot woman
who slapped your butt upside down came home
yesterday with brand new twin boys look just like you.
And that uncle who boots you used to polish
sent out a letter sayin' he leavin' you everything he got.

Funny how life stab one cheek then kiss the other.
We can cry for years but sometimes gotta smile too.
You want this handkerchief I just blew my nose on?
Since we cryin' here together boy I'll give it to you for free.

Alvin and the Youth

He bangs his head
     against iron fences of ignorance,

looks like me at his age
     banging my head against something similar',

but he got it worse got it bad
     the boy got it fucked up no good at all.

Pain and blood always told me when to stop
     but his fence harder and he seem to kind'a like the
pain,

kind'a like the blood, like the merry-go-round of hate
     cuttin' zeros all over his brain.

He slams his heart
     on the concrete of arrogance,

looks like a baby black eagle
     still too nekkid to fly straight or strong,

but he got it worse the boy got it bad got it bad
     he got it all fucked up and way past no good.

The wind and instinct will tell a baby eagle
     he gotta keep his ass still,

but you ignore the wind
     and you curse your instinct,

you seem to kind'a like the danger, sho' nuff dig the fear

kind'a like the drugged-out crazy eyes of death
kneeling between your bony knees pointing to his mouth,

you seem to be absolutely certain
      that raping your soul will somehow taste divine.

Tattoo Blues for My Lover the Junkie

On her tits stand two wide-fanned palm trees
that drop coconuts in my nude lap
whenever she sneezes love or giggles sorrow.
The needle tracks on her right arm
are pilgrims going up a holy mountain
circled with smoke rings of dead time.
Inside her dreams of blood-tongued haikus
we suck night through each others' mouths and blow
bubbles of stars in the face of the moon.

Both of her thighs tattooed with a flying phallus
that jumps hard when her muscles flex or when
mine lines up hungrily between the two of hers.
To the death-waltz of tanks in Iraq and the
mad-ghoul shrieks of shredded brains in Israel
we explode geometric crystals of junkie oohs
and ahhs, and ohh-myyy-Gawwwds!!!

Inside my sleep of needle-scarred sun-downs
we groove on the courage it takes for E
to consistently equal MC/Square.
Occasionally our faith fails and we
croon our reds, whites, and blues:

"Fix me good baby, baby fix me right,
fix me in the morning, fix me all night.
Don't know how I caught all this shit and fear,
wasn't broke a bit when I first got here.
You gotta fix me baby, said baby make me right."

Bright Kiss of Insanity

With intellect and beauty locked away
inside liquid chapels of candle-lit madness,
yours remain the eyes that fed Solomon
his wisdom. And the celestial garden of your face
the same for which a thousand moons buried
their crumbled hearts beneath a trembling sea.

Like the satin flower scent of a coffin your gaze
thickens before the danger of swords. Or love.
And like the obscene image of a demon's corpse
sniffing its crotch for fresh food
you stalk joy's temple with malicious fatal sorrow.

Who can prove this is punishment from God?
Who would want to? Why hang so many signs
claiming Jesus was preoccupied the day paradise
died in your smile and turned your springtime lips
into a land oppressed by cruel endless winter?

To slaughter beauty and suckle hypocrisy—
sport for maniacs and apocalyptic ghouls.
What hell condemned, let heaven now heal.
A girl like you: your platinum heart ground up like
beef, devoured and shat by the canines of bigotry
   and hate.

Nevermore the furious glory of your mind at work
stitching luminous tapestries of revelation and grace.
Laugh loud, my summer-poem darling, and sing now
too, for insanity's bright kiss shines blessings divine
upon angels so wondrous and tortured as you.

The Earth in Rapture, Our Earth

The Earth in rapture sings a holy hurricane
of ten thousand prophet-poets
burning stones and blood to the music
of higher rainbow spheres, every leaping tree
declares itself a divine idiot dancing inside
shadows of history and flames of tomorrow.

Our Earth in rapture screams the muted glory
of a shy goddess wed to ecstasy and destiny.
Her veil of tidal waves and indigo clouds
hide scalding tears of smoke and lava.
Volcano rumblings of cosmic grief
moan soft blue thunder as she re-births
her eternal rhythms of eternal love.

Page from a Red Scream Burned in Translation

Not your touch but your overloaded need
chained the world's tongues to legends
of blood-smeared gold and iron tears.
Your souls broke like the planet's heart,
drew us up from the dead waters
of your lives' sudden insanity,
tumbled our apathy like burned bones
across the void of our bleeding names and faces.

We sat on cliffs of twilight overlooking hell,
struggling to dream ourselves blind
over the orgy of the furies of 2005:
the tsunami that ate humans raw,
the howling that raped Haiti numb,
twin hags Katrina and Rita tripped out on heroine,
the pornographic disease of terrorism and war,
and this earthquake that snapped the camel's skinless back.

As if the frozen geometry of heaven's sorrow
multiplied and spread like a tribe of wandering orphans.
The atomic white horror oozing in and out
of naked and bewildered humanity
stuffs our mouths with the scabbed flesh
of prophecies dipped in honey and acid.
Out of light and unseen years, we moan new beginnings
that no one has promised, and no one delivered.

A Poem That Knew No Better

With rhymes of lesser distinction and themes lit
By dubious intentions, I was born blood-wet and red
To the tears of a broken pen and the smile of an
    abused angel.

Dressed up in sonnets, happily nude in open verse,
I fluttered iridescent pages of faith, hope, and charity
Through tornado screams of one world's challenged soul.

For I was a poem that knew no better,
    wandering then, wandering now.

Upon the lips of babes asleep I saw light embracing light
And so allowed my syllables to rest there as a prayer
They might sing in their dreams, or let drool across
    their cheeks.

Wandering then, wandering now, I was a poem
    that knew no better.

Within the bosoms of mothers and wives and
    husbands of soldiers,
I saw the earth crack like madness in a stone god's
    drunken rage,
And for them, with crystal lines built my trembling bridge.

For I, a poem lost in this strange world, never knew
    any better.

Humbly I presented my pages as silk-laced tissue at a
banquet— for warlords and terrorists, and I begged

my belligerent brothers, "Get thee thine shit together please,
as truly it makes life most foul."

Due to the nature of my being, I knew not better.

Where the eyes of lovers prayed, I was prone to
sparkling joy.
Where the garden of grace blossomed, star-scented
moonlight made me drunk.
Where the oceans of heaven sighed peace, I flowed
into a midnight wave of echoes.

For I was a poem that knew no better,
wandering then, wandering now.

Acknowledgments

For their inspiration, encouragement and support of my work during the writing of *Visions of a Skylark Dressed in Black*, I am deeply grateful to the following individuals and organizations:

The good souls, past and present, at *ESSENCE Magazine:* Susan Taylor, Diane Weathers, Cynthia Gordy, and Angela Kinamore, who blessed my life with the publication of: *Every Hour Henceforth* (along with *Family Reunion: Remembering the Ancestors,* from my first book) in the magazine's December 1999 *End-of-the-Century Collector's Edition; DarkMagusMilesAhead #7* in the January 2003 issue; and *Botanical Gardens #2* along with *In a Quiet Place on a Quiet Street* in the May 2005 *35th Anniversary Collector's Edition of Essence.* Moreover, I'm honored to say that *ESSENCE* published throughout 2005 a number of poems not included in this volume. In June 2006, the magazine published *My One Favorite City.*

My good brother Luther E. Vann, whose creative spiritual visions continue to inspire my own and whose paintings provided several of the poems in this book with their titles: *Fulton Street/the Series; Alvin and the Youth; All in a Day's Work; The Seeker,* and *Botanical Gardens #2.*

Michele Wood, whose painted universe reminded a wounded skylark that he still had songs worth singing and inspired a good number of these poems.

The mega-talented Roy LaGrone, whose painting,

DarkMagusMilesAhead #7, called out loudly enough for me to hear and respond with a poem in its name.

The former *Savannah Literary Journal* editorial board: for its extensive support of my work, and particularly for awarding *Sweet Brother Beat-Bop Daddy K* its Irene Tromble McAlister Literary Prize for the year 2000.

Sister Vaughnette Goode, whose monthly open mic at Savannah's Gallery Espresso gave me yet one more reason to keep on keeping on.

The staff at *Connect Savannah* for their generous recognition of my work and the publication of *Gratitudes of a Dozen Roses* during a very special National Poetry Month 2002.

At a time when I was certain I had written all the poetry I ever would, the very supportive and gifted online literary communities known as AuthorsDen, Blogit.com, and later Creative Thinkers International empowered me with their camaraderie and by sharing their own amazing works.

To all of the above and to every soul that ever uttered a prayer or entertained a positive hope on behalf of another: Thank You!

Aberjhani
Savannah, GA
Summer 2012

About the Author

A member of P.E.N. American Center and the American Academy of Poets, the Savannah, Georgia-born writer Aberjhani is the recipient of numerous awards for his works in multiple genres. These include: the CONNECT SAVANNAH 2006 Readers Poll for Best Poet and Spoken Word Artist; Writing Forum Poet of Month January 2007; the Choice Academic Title Award for *Encyclopedia of the Harlem Renaissance*, (co-authored by Sandra L. West); the Thomas Jefferson Journalism Award; a bronze medal for the Freedom Foundation essay competition; and the Michael Jackson VIP Portrait Dot Award for his "Looking at the World through Michael Jackson's Left Eye" series. He made his national debut as an author with a cover story for *ESSENCE* Magazine in 1997 and continued to publish poetry in the periodical for the next decade.

The author stands among a handful of modern writers who continuously garner recognition for expanding and reshaping the boundaries of literary expression. He studied journalism and creative writing at: Savannah State University; Eckerd College in St. Petersburg, Fla.; Macalester College in St. Paul, Minn.; Temple University in Philadelphia; and the New College of California in San Francisco. He served his writing apprenticeship as a U.S. Air Force military journalist in Alaska for two years and Great Britain for four years.

In addition to winning major awards, his *Encyclopedia of the*

Harlem Renaissance was listed *by Black Issues Book Review* as one of its "essential reference books for the home library." He is also editor and co-author of *The Wisdom of W.E.B. Du Bois*, as well as author of *I Made My Boy Out of Poetry*. He released his first spoken word cd, *The Goddess and the Skylark*, with fellow poets Nordette Adams and "Rahkyt" in 2006. In 2007, he completed his first novel, *Christmas When Music Almost Killed the World*, which he describes as a southern blues-gospel rock opera.